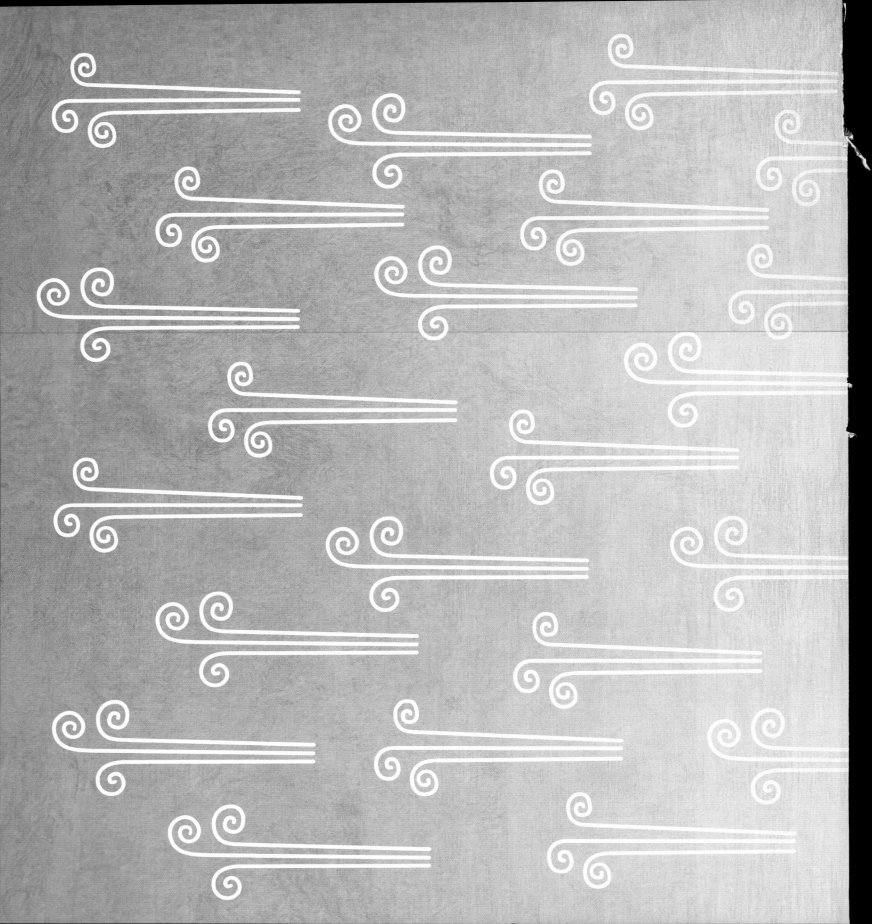

CHILD OF THE FLOWER-SONG PEOPLE

Luz Jiménez, Daughter of the Nahua

WRITTEN BY
GLORIA AMESCUA

ILLUSTRATED BY
DUNCAN TONATIUH

ABRAMS BOOKS FOR YOUNG READERS

NEW YORK

The images in this book were hand drawn and then collaged digitally.

Cataloging-in-Publication Data has been applied for and may be obtained from the Library of Congress.

ISBN 978-1-4197-4020-6

Text copyright © 2021 Gloria Amescua
Illustrations copyright © 2021 Duncan Tonatiuh
Edited by Howard W. Reeves
Book design by Heather Kelly

Printed and bound in China
10 9 8 7 6 5 4 3 2 1

Abrams Books for Young Readers are available at special discounts when purchased in quantity for premiums
and promotions as well as fundraising or educational use. Special editions can also be created to specification.
For details, contact specialsales@abramsbooks.com or the address below.

ABRAMS THE ART OF BOOKS
195 Broadway, New York, NY 10007
abramsbooks.com

For my parents, Anacleto and Antonia,
and my granddaughters, Ruby and Violet —G.A.

To Patty with all my love. Thank you for being my partner
in this crazy adventure —D.T.

A girl stared at the stars sprinkling the hammock of sky.
Like many other nights she listened to the
        whisperings of the ancient Aztecs in the wind.
        She heard their *xochicuicatl*, their flower-song.
She listened as the elders repeated tales their grandfathers had told.
Tales their grandfathers' grandfathers had told:
        how sacred streams and mountains protect them,
                how the Nahua lost their land to Cortés, the conqueror,
        and to the Spaniards who followed him.

She was Luz Jiménez,
child of the flower-song people,
the powerful Aztecs,
    who called themselves Nahua—
        who lost their land, but who did not disappear.

In Milpa Alta, a village slung between two mountains,
Luz's father harvested maguey and corn.
She watched closely as her mother taught her
how to grind corn in a metate,
how to twist yarn with her toes,
how to weave on a loom.

Luz was curious about everything—
which mushrooms were good to eat
and which would make you sick,
which popote could be brooms,
which herbs medicine.

She hummed as she worked, words
glowing and swirling in her head
in the Aztec language, Nahuatl.
This was life for the Nahua,
and Luz soaked it all in.

Evenings by the fire, Luz listened eagerly to stories about
the Mountain Boy, Tepozton, the son of a god—
how he never missed when he shot quail and turkey for the people to eat,
    how he hung bells on a steeple no one could reach,
        and how he outwitted a man-eating giant!
    And how Malintzin, betrayer of the Aztecs,
        was swept to the top of a mountain,
    where she cries in the wind at night,
        pulling her long black hair.

Luz wove all these old stories into her heart.
Through them she tasted bitter sorrow—
    how the Nahua suffered—
and sweet joy—
    how her people survived.
Luz was a child of the flower-song people.

Mornings on the way to market,
Luz and her mother passed a teacher's house,
students bent over reading.
Luz carried an empty place inside. She yearned to know
what was written on the papers.
A secret longing began to bud in her heart.
The secret fluttered lightly like wings in her chest.
    She would study hard.
        She would learn what the squiggles meant.
            She would learn to read!

But Luz, like the other native people,
was a forgotten shadow
to those who governed. There was no
public school for them.

Mornings,
Luz learned from Spanish schoolbooks.
Afternoons,
she studied dressmaking, drawing, and baking bread,
not the corn tortillas of her people.
Luz excelled and won many prizes,
and her voice sparkled as she told Nahua stories in secret to other children.
If the students spoke Nahuatl instead of Spanish,
    the teachers punished them.
They had to give up their Nahua clothes, wear modern ones like in the cities.
The budding flower in Luz's heart might have withered.
    But it did not.

These new rules were changing the Nahua,
but Luz was different.
    She longed to blossom,
        carrying the beautiful traditions of her people with her.

Luz found strength in remembering how old Teuhtli, not wanting to let his daughter go,
    turned her and the young man she loved into mountains—
        Iztaccíhuatl, Sleeping Lady, and Popocatépetl, Smoking Mountain.
    How the mountains protected the people and brought precious rain.
    Luz was a child of the flower-song people.
    She wanted to protect the Nahua ways.

Her body tingling, Luz spilled her secret to very few,
"I want to be a teacher when I grow up."
Her secret yearning was beginning to bloom,
imagining teaching future generations.
But at thirteen,
    her dreams whirled away in a storm . . .

The Mexican Revolution came to Milpa Alta.
Soldiers stole their food.
They burned her precious home and school to rubble.
Her father, like nearly all of the men, was shot and killed.
Luz and her mother and sisters fled to Mexico City at night,
stars lighting the way. Others followed.

Luz said, "Not a soul was left . . ."

In the large, unfamiliar city clogged with too many sounds, smells, and people,
the widows and girls struggled to make a living.
They sold homemade atole, tamales, or handicrafts.
But Luz, with growing strength, opened up to something much different for a Nahua.

She found a job posing for artists drawn
to her strong features—
her sturdy body, her large dark eyes.

As she posed, she taught them the gifts she had learned from her beginnings—
grinding corn in a metate,
twisting yarn with her toes,
weaving on a loom.
Luz was a natural model and teacher. She understood what the artists needed without being told.

Artists until then had painted the Spanish heritage of Mexico—
the light-skinned Europeans and their religious beliefs—
but these artists of the twentieth century
honored the native people
who had been colonized by the Spanish,
stripped of their language and culture,
shamed and mistreated.

Luz represented her people well

through her indigenous features,

her skills, and

being true to her roots.

Luz became the most well-known model in all of Mexico for artists like
Diego Rivera, Fernando Leal, Tina Modotti, Jean Charlot, and others.
Painters painted.
Photographers clicked.
Sculptors carved.

The world recognized the beauty and strength of the native people
after five hundred years of being in shadows.
Through Luz, the world came to know
"the spirit of Mexico."

Though many artists sought out Luz,
her heart still longed to teach.

After the Revolution, Luz returned to Milpa Alta
and applied to be a teacher.

But, without being given a reason, Luz was rejected.
Once again, her dream seemed to swirl away forever
like petals on the wind.

But in the city she had become friends with artists and scholars.
    These scholars wanted to learn Nahua culture.
    They wanted to learn Nahua language.
    They wanted to go to Milpa Alta.

So Luz at last became a teacher,
    weaving the threads of her
    flower-song, *xochicuicatl*—
    her language and culture—
    into their hearts.

Eagerly, she led anthropologists and artists on tours of Milpa Alta.
There she showed them
  how the Nahua knew good mushrooms from bad,
    which popote made strong brooms,
      how they used herbs for medicine.

Luz also took them to Chalma,
where the visitors watched native festival dancers
and worshipers who had walked for days to place candles or flowers at the church.
Luz brought to life the world of the native Mexican people
and their pride in their culture and roots.

Inspired by Luz's teachings,
   the artists painted.
    The scholars wrote.
Luz was a powerful woman of the
  flower-song people.
Luz told her tales to a college professor,
Fernando Horcasitas, an anthropologist.
He wrote down what she patiently told him
in Nahuatl,
   word-by-word,
     phrase-by-phrase,
     week-by-week.

Luz was a "living link" to the Aztecs,
her words published in books to teach future generations
    the language of her people.
Professor Horcasitas asked her to help him teach
Nahuatl at the College of Mexico City.

Like the mountains, Iztaccíhuatl and Popocatépetl,
she protected the dying Nahua culture.
Her memories were some of the precious few written
in the lively voice of one of their own
as it was disappearing in the wind.

At long last, Luz's heart bloomed fully.
Her dream of being a teacher had come true,
      true in more ways than the young girl gazing at the sprinkled stars
          could have ever imagined.
Just by being Nahua,
      just by being herself,
Luz breathed life into *xochicuicatl*, the flower-song of the Nahua,
      and carried their fading voice into the future.

AUTHOR'S NOTE

"I have seen many good things and many bad things in my life,
but what I loved most was when I was a little girl and started going to school."

—Luz Jiménez

Julia Jiménez, later known as Luz Jiménez (Loos Hee-MEH-nes), came from a Nahua (NAH-wah) family in Milpa Alta, Mexico. Despite many obstacles in her life, she succeeded in being the teacher she always dreamed of becoming by honoring her culture.

At the University of Texas at Austin, I found a pamphlet announcing a symposium about Luz Jiménez in 2000, and I was immediately fascinated. Unfortunately, the meeting had already passed, but I kept the pamphlet anyway. In 2013, I wrote my first draft of this manuscript. I was drawn to Luz Jiménez, as both a teacher and as a Latina who grew up in Texas almost losing my Spanish language and culture. I've had to work at regaining both.

When we look at art that depicts a person, we rarely consider the real person behind the model. In 1997, a special exhibition in Mexico City focused on Luz Jiménez. This exhibit of paintings, drawings, sculptures, and photographs featured works by some of the most famous artists of the twentieth century who had lived and worked in Mexico: Fernando Leal, Diego Rivera, David Alfaro Siqueiros, Jean Charlot, Tina Modotti, and Edward Weston. All the art depicted Luz. Images of Luz are world-famous and appear in great murals in national buildings in Mexico City, hang in museums around the globe, and are sold as prints. Luz never sought the limelight and remained humble all her life. It took a lot of courage for her to become a model. She never told her mother about her modeling work. It wasn't something that Nahua women typically did.

Luz knew how to communicate her traditional Nahua upbringing through art and her native language. The Nahua called poetry *xochicuicatl*, "the flower and the song" (*floricanto* or *flor y canto* directly translated into Spanish). I use the term "flower-song" to represent the Nahua spirit in Luz and the Nahua people.

Into the early twentieth century Nahua still spoke Nahuatl (NAH-wah-tul) and carried on many of their ancient traditions. Officials believed the native people held back progress in Mexico and sought to change the culture and language of the indigenous people. They jailed fathers if they or their families did not follow the new rules. As a result, younger generations began losing their language and customs. Around the world, including the United States, conquering nations systematically have shamed indigenous speakers and tried to erase their culture in many ways. Luz's legacy is helping new generations to treasure their native traditions.

I appreciate Dr. Kelly McDonough at the University of Texas at Austin, whose work on Luz Jiménez has been invaluable and who introduced me to Luz's grandson, Jesús Villanueva Hernández. I am very grateful to them both for generously sharing resources and for their support.

ARTIST'S NOTE

Some of the illustrations in this book are inspired by works of art for which Luz Jiménez modeled. These I note below. I want to give special thanks to Jesús Villanueva—Luz's grandson—for his expertise and for sharing with me resources that clarified what artworks Luz posed for. Jesús is committed to sharing his grandmother's story and to preserving her legacy. I hope this book contributes to that effort and that it helps young readers learn about Luz's extraordinary life.

Luz Jiménez modeling for artists Ramón Alva de la Canal, Fernando Leal and Francisco Díaz de León at the Escuela de Pintura al Aire Libre de Coyoacán (School of Outdoor Painting in Coyoacán), 1920. Photographer unknown.

Jacket cover and page 29:
Fernado Leal
India con frutas, 1920
Oil on canvas
Fernando Leal Audirac Collection

Page 5 (title page):
Diego Rivera
La maestra rural, 1923
Fresco mural
Mexico City
Secretariat of Public Education first floor

Page 26:
Diego Rivera
La Molendera, 1924
Encaustic on canvas
Museo Nacional de Arte / INBA Collection

Page 28:
Diego Rivera
Indigena tejiendo, 1936
Oil on Canvas
Phoenix Art Museum Collection

Page 39:
José María Urbina
Fuente de los Cántaros
Mexico City
Parque México, Condesa.

TIMELINE

1897

Julia Jiménez González (Luz Jiménez) is born in Milpa Alta, a small farming community, on January 28.

1904–1908

Luz is a student at Elementary School #4 and Concepción Arenal Upper Primary School.

1911–1914

During the Mexican Revolution, Milpa Alta is at the center of the fight between the Zapatistas, led by revolutionary fighter Emiliano Zapata, and federal soldiers. Luz's school is burned down in 1914.

1916

Venustiano Carranza's men kill Luz's father and uncles and most of the men and boys in the massacre in Milpa Alta. Luz and her family leave Milpa Alta to live in Santa Anita on the edge of Mexico City.

1918–1919

Luz wins first place for the "Loveliest Flower of the Field," an indigenous beauty contest in Santa Anita. She takes the name Luciana for the contest and later goes by Luz.

1920–1965

Luz models for many famous artists working in Mexico throughout her lifetime.

1924–1925

Luz takes Anita Brenner (writer), Jean Charlot (artist), and others to the Sanctuary of Chalma.

1929–1965

Benjamin Lee Whorf (a North American linguist), Mariano Silva y Aceves, Robert Barlow, Stanley Newman, Fernando Horcasitas, and others studying Nahuatl use Luz's talents as a Nahuatl speaker. Throughout her life, Luz continues to model and also sells clothing and other articles that she and other women create to sustain herself and her family.

1936

Luz applies to the Secretariat of Education to be a rural school teacher but is rejected.

1940

Milpa Alta hosts the First Aztec Congress, which mainly determines what written Nahuatl should look like.

1942

Luz narrates stories that Anita Brenner edits and Jean Charlot illustrates, *The Boy Who Could Do Anything & Other Mexican Folk Tales*. Luz does not receive her promised one third of the profits of this book.

1950

Luz writes several essays in Nahuatl, which are published in Robert Barlow's Nahuatl-language newspaper, *Mexihcatl Itonalama*.

1956

Fernando Horcasitas and Luz teach students Nahuatl at the College of Mexico City.

1957

Luz relates stories to Anita Brenner that become the book, *Juan el tonto y los Banditos* (*Dumb Juan and the Bandits*), illustrated by Jean Charlot.

1961

The national daily newspaper *Excélsior* publishes an article about Doña Luz's life, and a television program *Working Women* interviews Luz.

1963

Horcasitas and Luz move to the Institute of Historical Research at the National University, where she recounts in Nahuatl the stories of Milpa Alta before and during the Revolution to their students.

1965

Luz Jiménez (Julia Jiménez) is hit by a car in Mexico City and dies on her 68th birthday, January 28th.

GLOSSARY

anthropologist: One who studies human races, societies, and cultures.

atole (ah-TOH-lee): A porridge made of corn flour.

Aztecs (AS-teks): A Mesoamerican culture that flourished from around 1300 to 1521. They are the Nahua's ancestors and consisted of several Nahuatl speaking groups. They did not use the term "Aztec" to refer to themselves.

maguey (mah-GAY): An agave plant.

Malintzin (mah-LEET-seen): Also known as Malinalli, Malinche, or Marina (c. 1501–c. 1529). An enslaved Popoluca woman, Malintzin acted as interpreter and advisor to conquering Spaniard Hernán Cortés and gave birth to his son.

metate (meh-TAH-teh): Flat grindstone.

popote (poh POH teh): Broom plant.

Teuhtli (TEWT-lee): Teuhtli is an extinct volcano that is one of the geographical boundaries and a symbol of Milpa Alta. There are many legends about the god it represents.

Tepozton (teh-POS-ton): Tepozton means "child of the mountain."

Xochicuicatl (shos-chee-KWEE-kah-tul): A Nahua word for poetry, which is translated literally as "floricanto" in Spanish and "flower-song" in English.

NOTES

Page 19: "Not a soul was left...." Jiménez, *Life and Death in Milpa Alta*, 177.

Page 25: "the spirit of Mexico." McDonough, *The Learned Ones*, 91.

Page 32: "living link." Charlot, *Jean Charlot and Luz Jimenez*, 2.

Page 39: "I have seen many good things and many bad things in my life, but what I loved most...." Jiménez, *Life and Death in Milpa*, 5.

See complete bibliography and more information on website: GloriaAmescua.com

SELECT BIBLIOGRAPHY

Charlot, John. "Jean Charlot and Luz Jiménez." Originally published as "Jean Charlot y Luz Jiménez." *Parteaguas* 2, no. 8 (Spring 2007). jeancharlot.org/writings-on-jc/john-charlot_jclj.html.

Jiménez, Luz. *Life and Death in Milpa Alta: A Nahuatl Chronicle of Díaz and Zapata*. Translated and edited by Fernando Horcasitas. Norman: University of Oklahoma Press, 1972.

Karttunen, Frances. "The Linguistic Career of Doña Luz Jiménez." *Estudios de Cultura Náhuatl* 30 (1999): 267–74. www.historicas.unam.mx/publicaciones/revistas/nahuatl/pdf/ecn30/595.pdf.

Luz Jiménez: Symbol of a Millennial People. Austin: MexicArte Museum, 2000. texashistory.unt.edu/ark:/67531/metapth304475/m1/2/.

McDonough, Kelly Shannon. "Indigenous Experience in Mexico: Readings in the Nahua Intellectual Tradition." PhD diss., University of Minnesota, 2010, 127–67. conservancy.umn.edu/handle/11299/93968.

McDonough, Kelly S. *The Learned Ones: Nahua Intellectuals in Postconquest Mexico*. Tuscon: University of Arizona Press, 2014, 120-153.

Villanueva, Jesús. "Doña Luz: Inspiration and Image of a National Culture." *Voices of Mexico*, no. 41 (October–December 1997): 19–24. www.revistascisan.unam.mx/Voices/pdfs/4105.pdf.